This book is a fiction book that helps readers learn math concepts through a fun story.

About the Author
Yoon Jeong Choi majored in early childhood education from Ehwa Women's University. She also won the grand prize from the MBC creative fairy tales tournament. Her books include *SaerokSaerok Interesting worldwide old tales, Creativity home-study materials Teach Coach, and You're Wonderful PpiyoPpiyo.*

About the Illustrator
Hyun Kyeong Shim studied at SI Illustration School and has been working as an illustrator since 2003. Her illustrations can be found in stories such as *Finding missing Daddy, The Button that popped, and Moon, Moon, What Kind of Moon.*

Tantan Publishing Knowledge Storybook **How to Avoid the Fearsome Cat**

www.TantanPublishing.com

Published in the U.S. in 2016 by TANTAN PUBLISHING, INC.
4005 w Olympic Blvd., Los Angeles, CA 90019-3258

©Copyright 2016 by Dong-hwi Kim
English Edition

ISBN: 978-1-939248-14-5

Printed in Korea

How to Avoid the Fearsome Cat

Written by Yoon Jeong Choi   **Illustrated by Hyun Kyeong Shim**

TanTan Publishing

In a small storage shed on the corner of a farm
lived fifteen mice. There was a blizzard outside the
window, but inside the shed was warm and cozy.
Every crate was filled with food.

One day, all the mice returned after playing
outside for a while.
The inside of the shed was all messed up.
"Take a look at this. There is a strange note!"

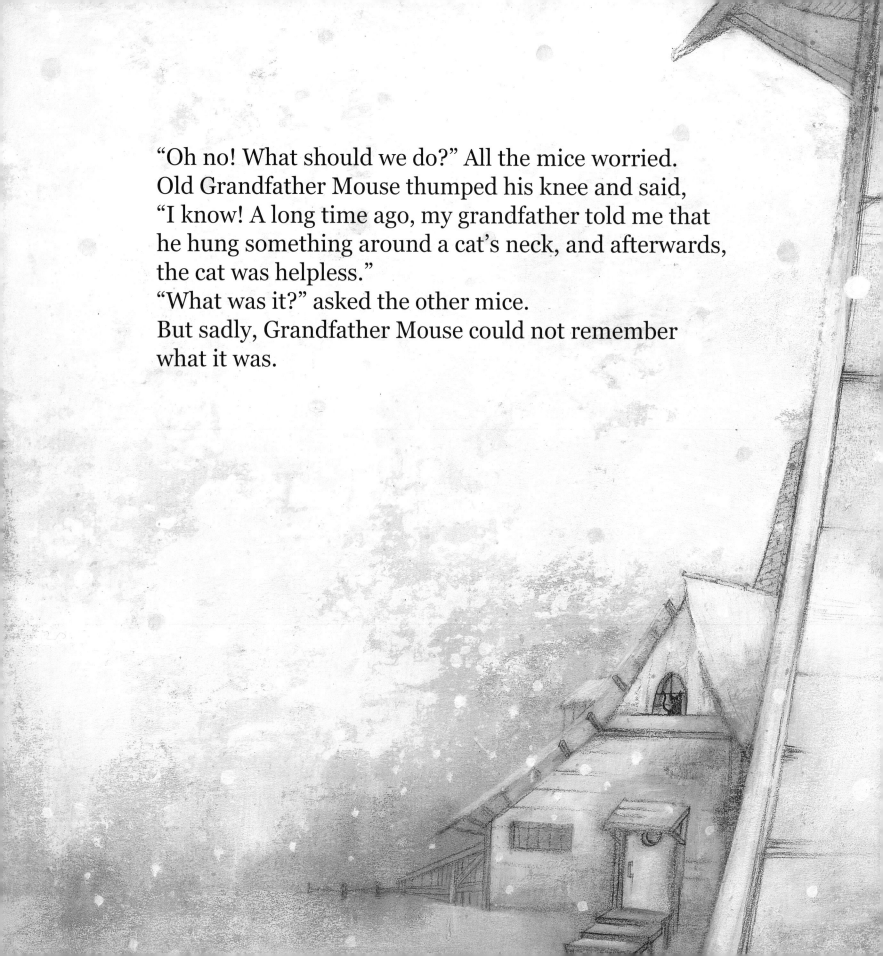

"Oh no! What should we do?" All the mice worried.
Old Grandfather Mouse thumped his knee and said,
"I know! A long time ago, my grandfather told me that
he hung something around a cat's neck, and afterwards,
the cat was helpless."
"What was it?" asked the other mice.
But sadly, Grandfather Mouse could not remember
what it was.

The mice held an emergency meeting.
The captain mouse spoke first.
"Everyone! What will be good to hang on a cat's neck?"
One mouse suggested, "Let's hang something heavy. So the cat won't be able to chase us!"
Another mouse worried, "Wouldn't it have to be light so we can carry it?"
The mice started to argue loudly.
"No, no, something heavy!"
"No, no, something light!"

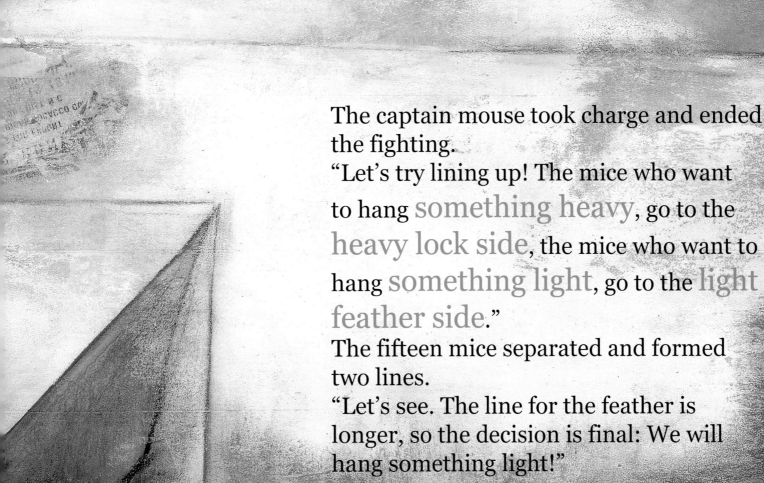

The captain mouse took charge and ended the fighting.

"Let's try lining up! The mice who want to hang something heavy, go to the heavy lock side, the mice who want to hang something light, go to the light feather side."

The fifteen mice separated and formed two lines.

"Let's see. The line for the feather is longer, so the decision is final: We will hang something light!"

The first step in a research survey is to sort the research objects; the mice sorted themselves into lines representing heavy or light. Next, count each item and draw a graph to organize them.

The captain mouse asked, "What should we choose among the light things?"
One mouse said, "Something that smells! Because we can sniff well."
Another suggested, "How about something that sparkles? It will be easy to see even during the dark nights."
A third mouse exclaimed, "Something that makes a sound! We will notice at once if the cat comes near."
In a panicked state, the mice formed into lines again but it was too disorganized.

The captain mouse grew impatient and brought out a sack of chestnuts.

"Let's take turns. Everyone place a chestnut in front of the item that you want to choose."

So the fifteen mice thumped, clumped, and stacked the chestnuts to mark their choices.

"The most chestnuts are placed by the whistle drawing.

So we have decided to use something that makes a sound!"

The whistle drawing received the most chestnuts. The whistle drawing stands for a thing that makes a sound. Including the previous decision, the mice have now decided to hang *something light and noisy*.

"Now, it is time to decide what to hang among the things that make sounds."

One mouse suggested, "What about a very loud alarm clock?"

The mouse captain replied, "Too noisy. A small bell would be just perfect."

The fifteen mice tried to place the chestnuts again, but the chestnuts kept falling and rolling away. So they came up with another idea.

Instead of using actual chestnuts, this time they decided to draw circles to represent the number of chestnuts.

After they were done, the captain mouse said, "There are more circles on this side,

So it is decided: We will hang a jingling bell."

"Now, who should hang the bell on the cat?"
Suddenly, the mice were very quiet.
No one dared volunteer to hang a bell on the ferocious cat's neck.
So the fifteen mice all came to the same conclusion, and shouted in unison, "It is decided: The farmer's wife will hang the bell!"

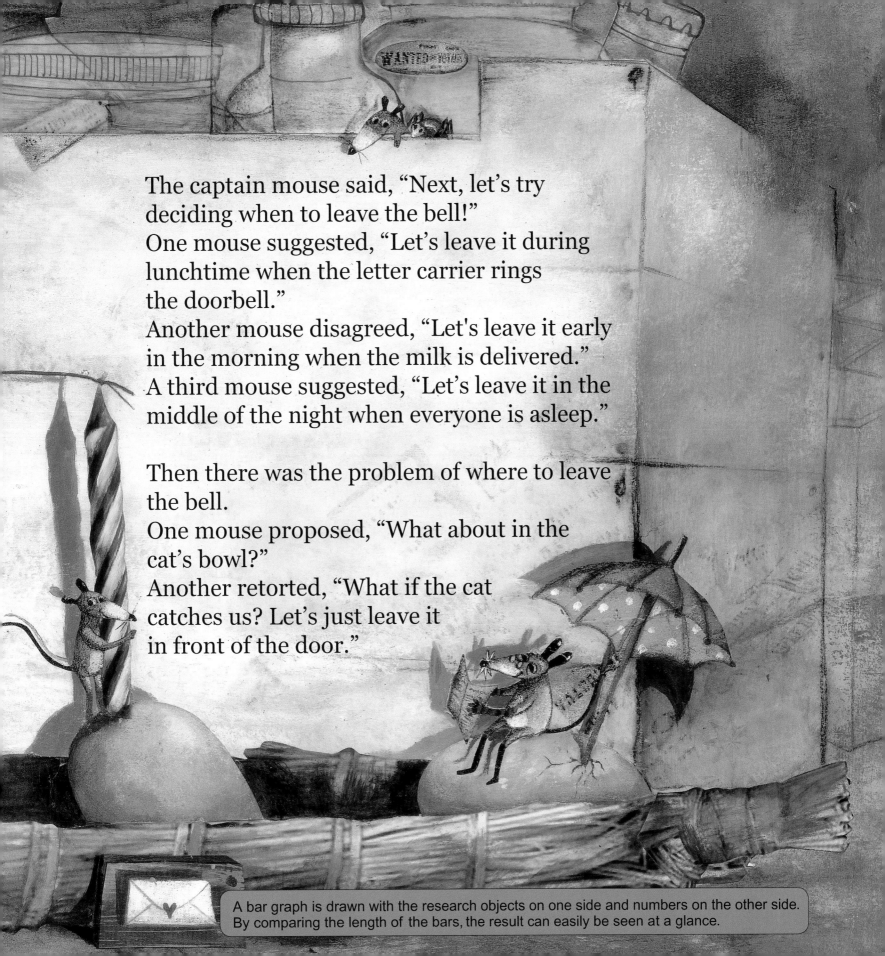

The captain mouse said, "Next, let's try deciding when to leave the bell!"
One mouse suggested, "Let's leave it during lunchtime when the letter carrier rings the doorbell."
Another mouse disagreed, "Let's leave it early in the morning when the milk is delivered."
A third mouse suggested, "Let's leave it in the middle of the night when everyone is asleep."

Then there was the problem of where to leave the bell.
One mouse proposed, "What about in the cat's bowl?"
Another retorted, "What if the cat catches us? Let's just leave it in front of the door."

A bar graph is drawn with the research objects on one side and numbers on the other side. By comparing the length of the bars, the result can easily be seen at a glance.

The fifteen mice were in agreement.
The mice raised their paws for each opinion that they favored, and they arranged their votes so it was easy to see at a glance.
"It is decided. We'll leave the bell at lunchtime when the letter carrier rings the doorbell! It is also decided that we'll leave it in front of the door!"

"Hurray, we're done!"
The mice found one bell
and wrapped it beautifully,
like a gift.

The next day at lunchtime,
the front door bell rang.
Ding-dong, ding-dong!
When the farmer's wife opened the door,
she looked down and saw a gift box.
She read the note.
"To the stylish and handsome cat?
Oh! Kitty, here's a gift for you!"

"Wow, a pretty bell. Do you like it?"
The farmer's wife hung the bell around the
cat's neck.
The cat was dreadfully displeased.
He rubbed and rubbed with his front paw.
And he tried shaking his neck to get the bell
off but, Jingle! Jingle! Jingle!

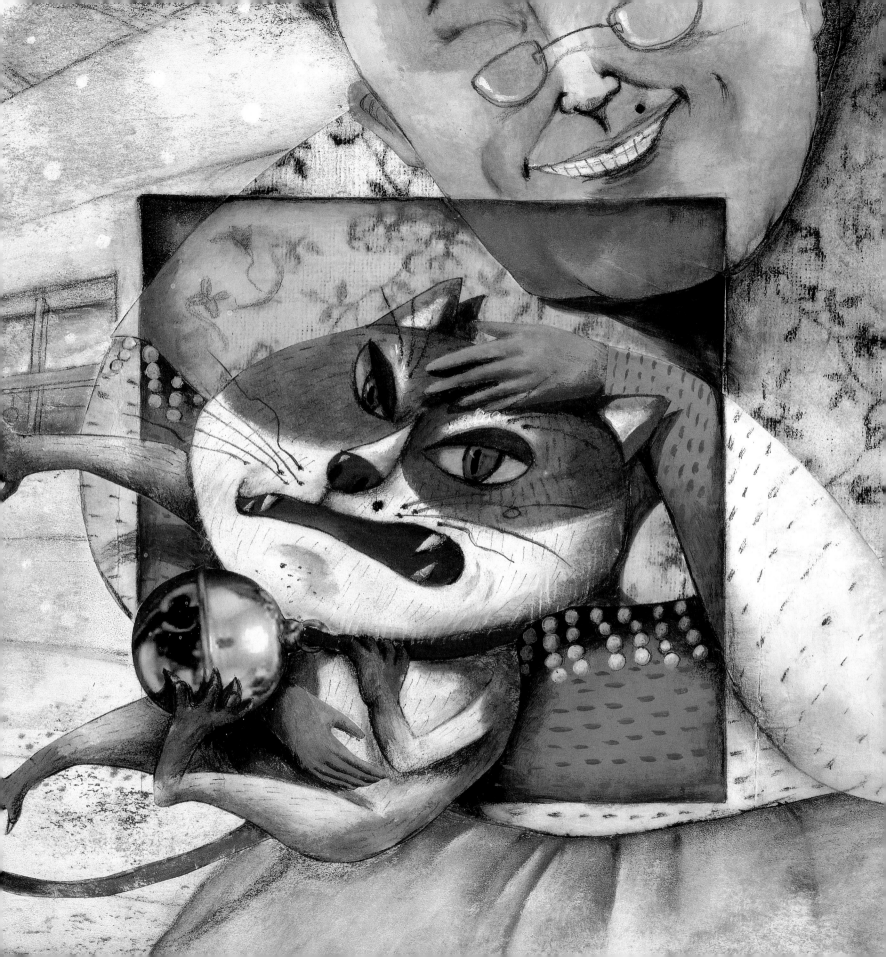

So from that day on, when the Jingle! Jingle! Jingle! Bell
rang, the mice rushed and hid in the yard and field.
The fifteen mice danced with triumph and ate all winter
until their bellies were full.

Graph and Mathematical thinking

Drawing a graph makes it easy to view the collected data at a glance, which is a part of a mathematical process called data organization. We gather the data to find the information and meaning contained in any situation in everyday life. This is called data collection. If you draw a graph, all the data collected can be understood easily and conveniently. However, organizing the data does not end here; data organization includes making any decision on the basis of the current data, or predicting what will happen in the future as well. Therefore, we can say that it provides opportunities for research and opportunities for interesting mathematical thinking.

In order for a child to successfully acquire these abilities, the child must be able to classify the collected data and compare the sizes and sequences of the resulting figures. Also the child needs to learn how to draw a bar graph that represents real objects or pictures. In everyday life with your child, you can try a variety of activities for collecting organizational data, such as weather, toys, clothes, or food.

Math 1st~2nd Grade > Tables and Graphs

Study Date _____ / _____

● **The diligent mice filled the food storage with dates, peanuts, and chestnuts.**

1. Count each item inside the sack and color the number of boxes for each food.

	1	2	3	4	5	6	7	8

2. Look at the table and determine whether there are the most dates, peanuts, or chestnuts inside the food storage.

_____

3. Color in the boxes to show the number of mice lined up in front of each favorite food. Use a different color for each food.

	1	2	3	4	5	6	7	8
🫐								
🥜								
🌰								

4. Between the dates, peanuts, and chestnuts, which is the mice's most favorite food?

_____

Study Date _____ / _____

● **The mice voted on who is the most popular mouse, what they are most afraid of, and what they would like to eat.**

1. Count how many votes each mouse received and write the correct number in the square.

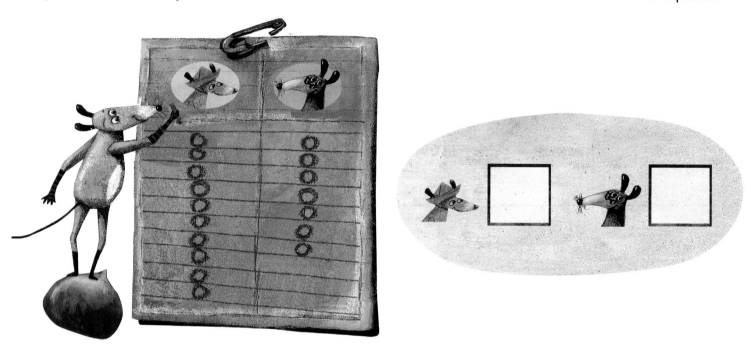

2. Based on the numbers you just wrote in the squares, identify the most popular mouse. Draw that mouse in the empty space below.

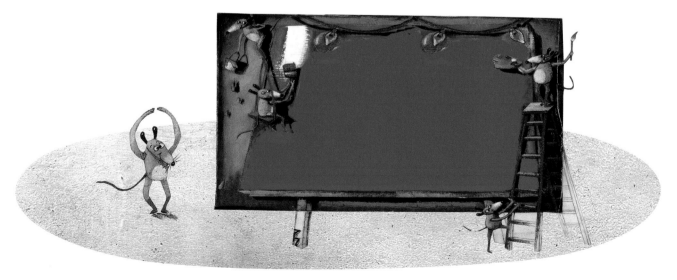

3. Look at the graph and write the correct number in the square.
   Then circle the correct word to complete each sentence.

The number of mice that are afraid of spiders ☐

The number of mice that are afraid of cats ☐

The mice are more afraid of (spiders / cats)

The number of mice that chose potatoes ☐

The number of mice that chose peppers ☐

The number of mice that chose radishes ☐

The mice most want to eat (potatoes / peppers / radishes).